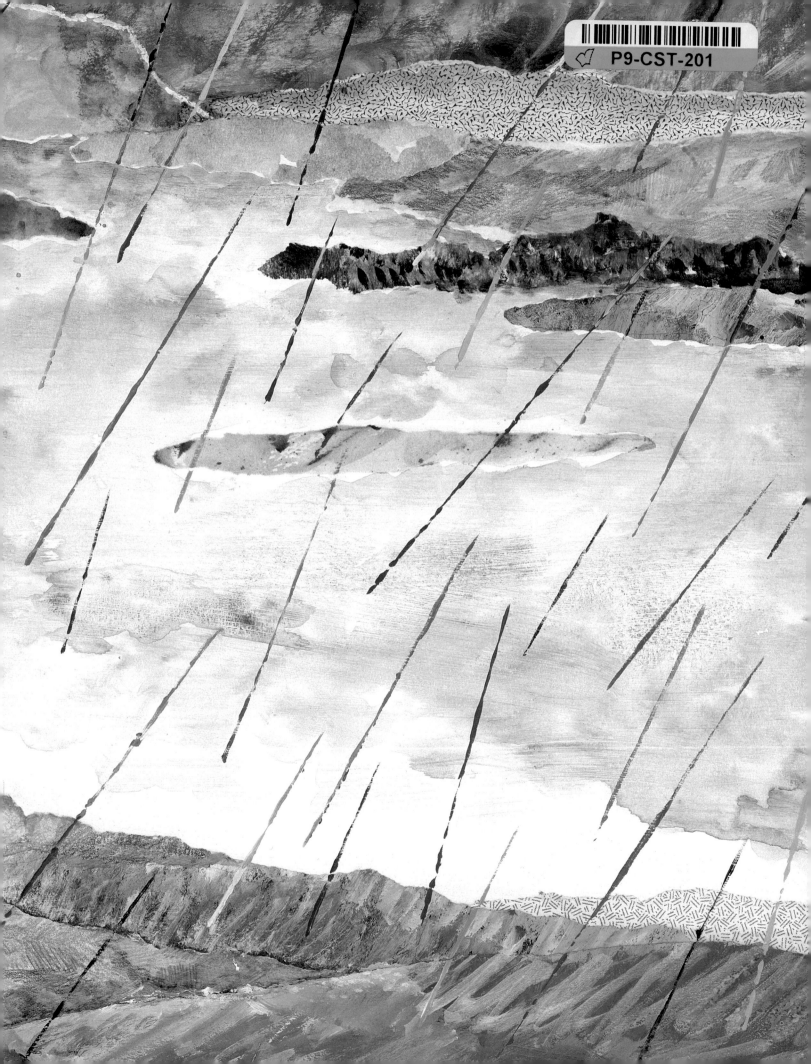

Zig

and the Magic Umbrella

Sylvie Kantorovitz

Dial Books for Young Readers
an imprint of Penguin Group (USA) LLC

For Barbara

DIAL BOOKS FOR YOUNG READERS

Published by the Penguin Group • Penguin Group (USA) LLC
375 Hudson Street • New York, New York 10014

USA / Canada / UK / Ireland / Australia / New Zealand / India / South Africa / China
penguin.com
A Penguin Random House Company

Text & pictures copyright © 2015 by Sylvie Kantorovitz

Library of Congress Cataloging-in-Publication Data • Kantorovitz, Sylvie, author, illustrator.
Zig and the magic umbrella / by Sylvie Kantorovitz. • pages cm • Summary: Zig, a small, blue creature who lives in a rainy,
gray world, grabs hold of a red umbrella and is carried away to a colorful forest where he becomes a hero—and a friend.
ISBN 978-0-8037-3913-0 (hardcover) • [1. Adventure and adventurers—Fiction. 2. Umbrella—Fiction. 3. Birds—Fiction.
4. Heroes—Fiction. 5. Friendship—Fiction.] I. Title. • PZ7.W6295Zig 2015 • [E]—dc23 • 2014006558

Manufactured in China on acid-free paper • 10 9 8 7 6 5 4 3 2 1

Designed by Maya Tatsukawa • Text set in SkippySharpCustom

The publisher does not have any control over and does not assume
any responsibility for author or third-party websites or their content.

The art was prepared in collage (with a variety of found and prepared papers) and acrylics on primed paper.

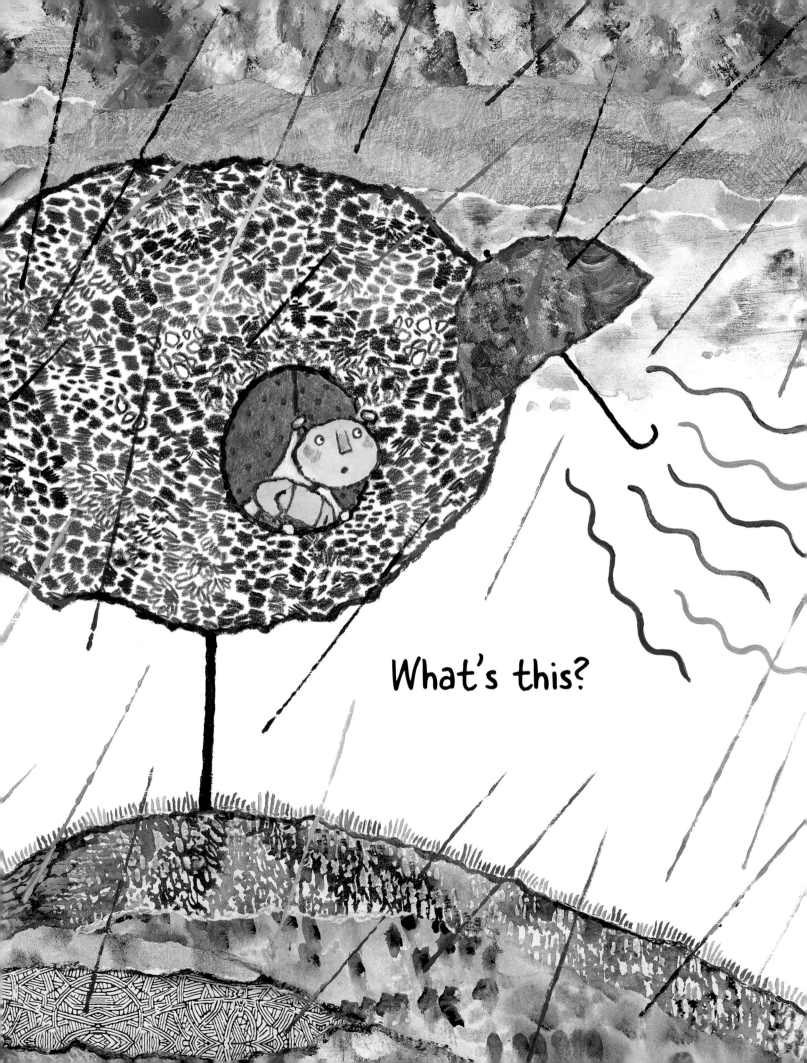

What's this?

Whoosh!

Whee...

Where am I going?

Wow!

Where are you
taking me, Bird?

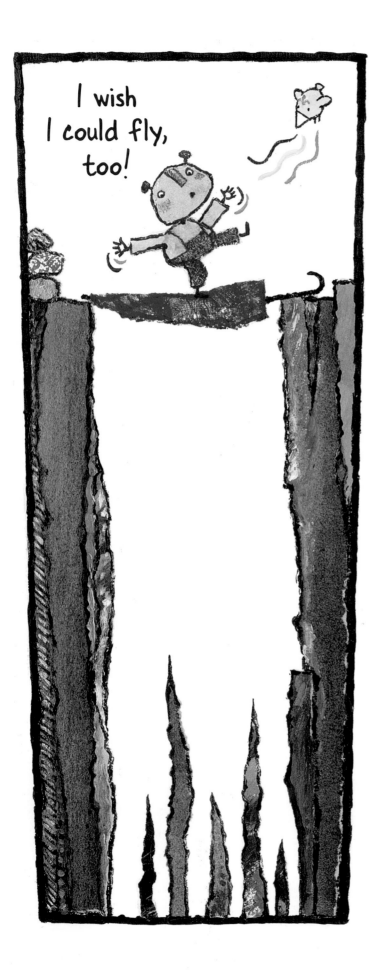

I wish
I could fly,
too!

shhh...

Time for me
to go home.
Good-bye,
Birds.

What do I see?

BIRD!

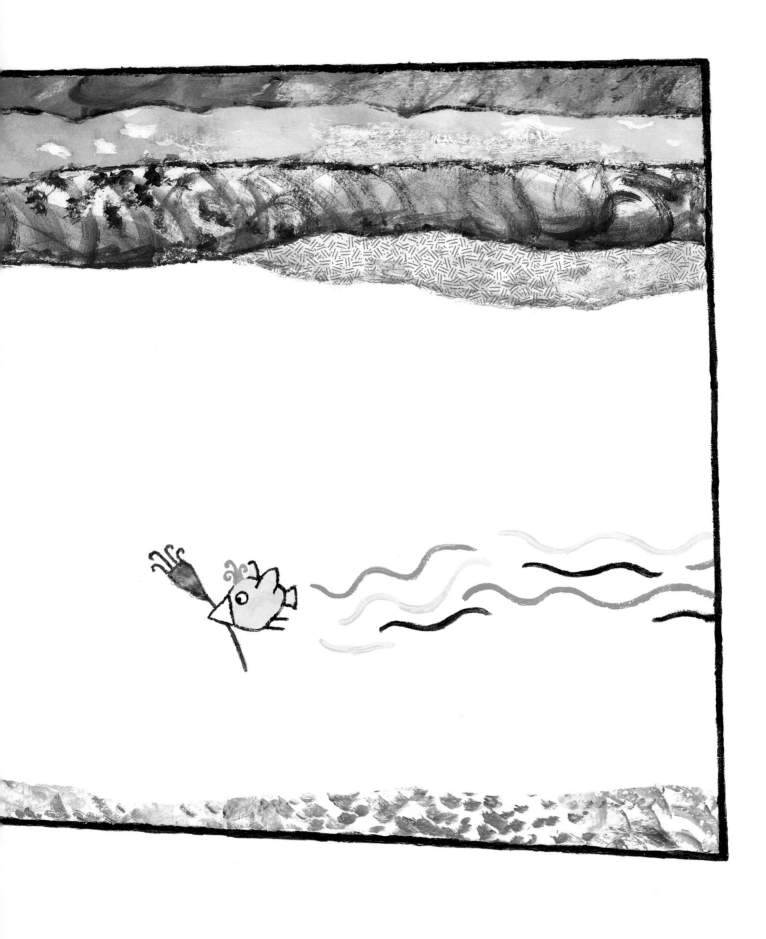